THE DUST BOWL

To Elsie, Marnie and Ann — DB
For John and Andrew — KR

For much of my knowledge and passion for this period, I am grateful
to the writers and historians Barry Broadfoot, James H. Gray,
Barnett Singer and Robert Goldston for their fine works about this
period, and to the articles "The Big Dry," which appeared in the
July 4, 1988, issue of *Time*, and "Great Plains III," which appeared in the
March 6, 1989, issue of *The New Yorker*. All served as inspiration and
as a rich source of information in the writing of this book.

Kids Can Press Ltd. acknowledges with appreciation
the assistance of the Canada Council and
the Ontario Arts Council in the production of this book.

Canadian Cataloguing in Publication Data
Booth, David
The dust bowl

ISBN 1-55074-295-7

1. Depressions – 1929 – Prairie Provinces – Juvenile fiction.
I. Reczuch, Karen. II. Title.

PS8553.067D8 1996   jC813'.54   C96-9300840

PZ7.B66Du 1996

The artwork in this book was rendered in graphite pencil
and watercolour on Lanaquarelle paper.

Kids Can Press Ltd.
29 Birch Avenue
Toronto, Ontario, Canada
M4V 1E2

Edited by Debbie Rogosin
Designed by Karen Powers

Printed in Hong Kong by
Wing King Tong Company Limited

96 0 9 8 7 6 5 4 3 2

THE DUST BOWL

Written by David Booth
Illustrated by Karen Reczuch

Kids Can Press Ltd.

Toronto

On Sunday morning, the wind blew outside the kitchen window. Matthew wiped the dust from his cereal bowl. He was used to removing the fine coating from everything in the house. It was almost as dusty inside as out. From the sideboard, the pictures of his mother and his grandma smiled at him.

When his father and his grandpa joined him at the table, they didn't say much, but he knew what they were thinking. Finally, he blurted out, "We aren't going to sell the farm, are we?"

His father set down his coffee mug and looked at Matthew's grandpa. "How much longer can we last, Pop?"

"As long as it takes," Grandpa answered.

"But the crops won't make it this year," his father snapped. "Without rain there'll be no grain. Without grain, there'll be no money."

Matthew said nothing. His grandpa stood up and walked over to the window. "The rain will come. The wheat will grow. It's not as bad as the last drought."

Matthew's father pushed his chair back angrily and went outside. He began to work in the small garden below the porch.

Matthew's grandpa sat down again, put milk and sugar in his tea
and began to talk.

"When your grandma and I first farmed this land, we were
young. We thought we had discovered gold in those fields of waving
wheat. The world needed wheat, and we wanted to grow enough of
it for everyone.

"We ploughed up all our land, even the field that we had decided not to seed yet. We borrowed from the bank and bought new equipment so we could plant as much wheat as possible. The prairies became a one-crop country.

"We needed luck, and the first year we found it. All the farmers did. The sun shone when it was supposed to, there was enough rain, the pests stayed away and the frost was late. Matthew, the prairies were covered with wheat.

"How fast things change on a farm! Just the next year, in mid-June, the crops were green and growing. But by July, the heat had burnt them down to nothing. When the sun took control it baked the land, and what rain there was could not soak into the ground. It was hot enough to fry your shoes. Too hot to work in the day, too hot to sleep at night. We harvested what we could, but your grandma and I began to worry.

"Then the rain stopped completely and times got worse. A hot sucking wind began to feed on the bare soil, and it blew the earth away. The grass that had fed the buffalo for centuries was no more.

"That wind blew for two solid weeks, blowing from the four corners of the world, blowing the land out from under our feet. It was the Big Dry. You had to see it to believe it, Matthew. It turned our world into a dust bowl. It blew open doors, broke windows and even flattened a barn or two.

"The dirt and the dust were everywhere. Your grandma stuffed towels in the crack at the bottom of the door to keep the dust out. When I went outside, I had to put a dish towel soaked in water over my nose and mouth. The dust drifted like snow against our fences, and even buried them sometimes. Children had to walk to school backwards to keep the wind-blown soil from stinging their faces. And when they got home, they had to clean the dust out of the nostrils of the cattle.

"And, oh, the dust clouds. How I remember them. Brown ones, red ones, yellow ones, made from the soil of thousands of farms across the prairies. One big dust cloud blocked out the sun for days. As it moved across the country it covered the land in darkness. We had to keep the lanterns lighted all day. Some people in the cities thought the end of the world had come.

"Your grandma could never get the laundry white. The curtains and the sheets were as grey as the sky. She scrubbed her fingers to the bone, but the dust kept winning. That's why we called those years the Dirty Thirties. Didn't beat your grandma, though. She fought the heat. She fought the wind. She fought the drought. Somehow she knew that she would see crops covering the fields with green again and the snow-white sheets billowing on the clothesline like great prairie schooners.

"A few of us farmers ploughed deep furrows around the fields to stop the earth from blowing away. Others thought it was hopeless to keep planting because their ploughs just turned up dry, fine dust that blew away in the wind. A few went to church and prayed for rain. For some, farming was becoming a slow way to starve."

Through the window, Matthew saw his father beginning to weed the little garden that his mother had planted before she died.

"I'm not saying we didn't consider giving up too, but we stayed. Things got better for a time, but wouldn't you know, two years later we were hit by nature one more time.

"Another cloud covered us — grasshoppers. They could black out the sun. Millions of them would stop all at once on a farm. They ate a crop in minutes, devouring every scrap of greenness. They even ate the bristles on the broom and the halter on the horse. When a train tried to run on tracks covered with grasshoppers, the wheels could get no traction, and they just spun around. Those insects could stop a train.

"The winter was the last straw for many farmers. It was colder than anyone could remember. We brought our mattresses into the kitchen at night to be near the heat of the cook-stove. The roads were so deep with snow that we couldn't go into town. We were cut off from everyone and everything.

"When many of my friends heard stories about the lush pickings on the west coast, they quit their farms. Tough farmers though they were, they left with their wives and kids, drained by heat and wind and cold and hardship. Chickens and everything else they owned were tied on the backs of the jalopies. Families were on the move. Schools were closed. The buildings were abandoned for good.

"Your father was born that year. We would put him on the bed between us and listen to the long whistles of the trains at night, heading west. I always loved that sound. Escape. We knew the trains were carrying farmers away from their land forever. But we couldn't leave, Matthew, we just couldn't leave. Some people's lives had dried up and blown away. But we stayed on our land and hung on to what little soil was left.

"Two years later, our land was alive again. It was green as far as the eye could see. The drought was over. The grasshoppers were gone. We were still farmers." His grandpa paused for a few moments. "That was fifty years ago, and the farm is still here. I could never have managed on my own after I lost your grandma, but your parents kept it going."

"Grandpa, is the Big Dry back?"

"I don't know, Matthew. I don't know."

They both stared out the window. The wind whistled, and swirls of dust danced across the fields.

Matthew went outside. His father put down the hoe, climbed the steps and sat beside him on the porch. They both stared at the bluest of skies. "I love this farm, Matthew. Your mother loved it too. She was afraid to live here at first, afraid of the space and all the quiet. But when she planted her garden, she became a part of this farm. She belonged here. You do too."

Matthew took his father's hand. "Will we have to sell the farm, Dad?"

Grandpa called out through the screen door, "The rain will come. If not this year, then next year. We can hang on."

Matthew looked at his father's face and saw a smile.

"All right, Pop," his father called. "We hear you."

Matthew felt warm inside. He looked up at the sky and thought the sun winked at him. Then Matthew and his father went back into the kitchen and sat down at the table with his grandpa. The three farmers ate their cereal and waited for rain.